W9-BFQ-237

STAR WARS®

THE CLONE WARS™

HERO OF THE CONFEDERACY
VOLUME THREE

THE DESTINY OF HEROES

SCRIPT
HENRY GILROY
STEVEN MELCHING

PENCILS
BRIAN KOSCHAK

INKS
DAN PARSONS

COLORS
MICHAEL E. WIGGAM

LETTERING
MICHAEL HEISLER

COVER ART
SCOTT HEPBURN WITH **MICHAEL E. WIGGAM**

A clash of titans! Separatist starfighter ace Tofen Vane shattered a Republic blockade of his home-world, Valahari. Embracing his role as liberator, he has spread his campaign throughout a wealthy region of the galaxy.

Desperate to stop this new hero of the Confederacy, the Jedi Council placed Anakin Skywalker in charge of a blockade to lure Tofen into attacking. Tofen took the bait, determined to get revenge on Anakin, the Jedi he believed responsible for his father's death.

During a fierce dogfight, both were shot down, and they confronted one another on the surface of an alien planet. Though Tofen got the upper hand, he stopped short of killing Anakin. However, he has promised that should they meet again, there will be no mercy . . .

Spotlight

DARK HORSE COMICS

Visit us at www.abdopublishing.com

Reinforced library bound edition published in 2011 by Spotlight, a division of the ABDO Group, 8000 West 78th Street, Edina, Minnesota 55439. Spotlight produces high-quality reinforced library bound editions for schools and libraries. Published by agreement with Dark Horse Comics, Inc., and Lucasfilm Ltd.

Printed in the United States of America, North Mankato, Minnesota.
102010
012011
This book contains at least 10% recycled materials.

Cataloging-in-Publication Data

Gilroy, Henry.
Hero of the Confederacy Vol. 3: the destiny of heroes / story, Henry Gilroy and Steve Melching ; art, Brian Koschak. --Reinforced library bound ed.
v. cm. -- (Star wars: the clone wars)
"Dark Horse Comics."
ISBN 978-1-59961-843-2 (v. 3)
1. Graphic novels. [1. Graphic novels.] I. Melching, Steve. II. Koschak, Brian, ill. III. Star Wars, the clone wars (television program) IV. Title.
PZ7.7.G55He 2011
741.5'973

Spotlight

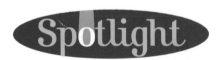

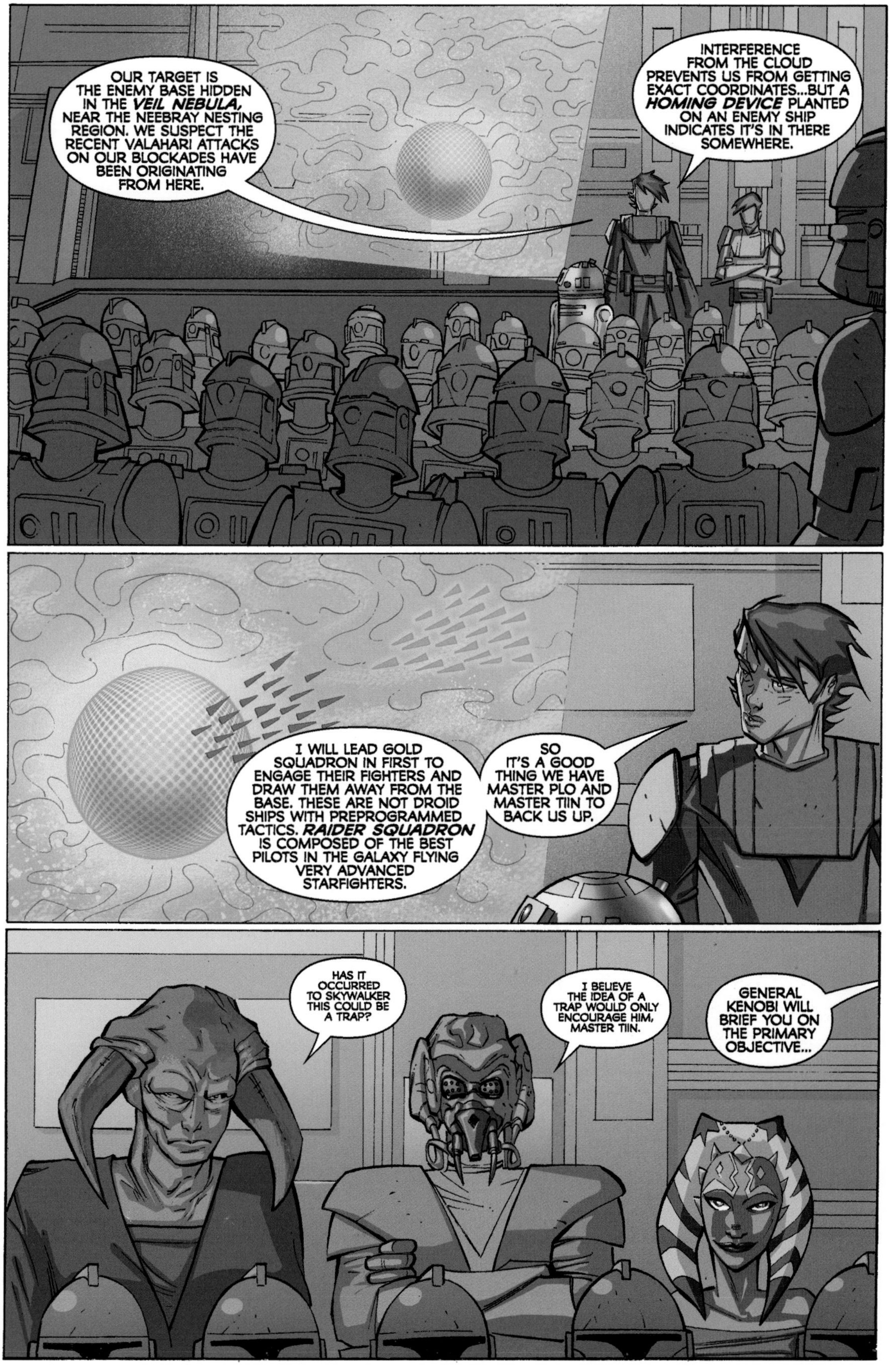
OUR TARGET IS THE ENEMY BASE HIDDEN IN THE VEIL NEBULA, NEAR THE NEEBRAY NESTING REGION. WE SUSPECT THE RECENT VALAHARI ATTACKS ON OUR BLOCKADES HAVE BEEN ORIGINATING FROM HERE.
INTERFERENCE FROM THE CLOUD PREVENTS US FROM GETTING EXACT COORDINATES...BUT A HOMING DEVICE PLANTED ON AN ENEMY SHIP INDICATES IT'S IN THERE SOMEWHERE.
I WILL LEAD GOLD SQUADRON IN FIRST TO ENGAGE THEIR FIGHTERS AND DRAW THEM AWAY FROM THE BASE. THESE ARE NOT DROID SHIPS WITH PREPROGRAMMED TACTICS. RAIDER SQUADRON IS COMPOSED OF THE BEST PILOTS IN THE GALAXY FLYING VERY ADVANCED STARFIGHTERS.
SO IT'S A GOOD THING WE HAVE MASTER PLO AND MASTER TIIN TO BACK US UP.
HAS IT OCCURRED TO SKYWALKER THIS COULD BE A TRAP?
I BELIEVE THE IDEA OF A TRAP WOULD ONLY ENCOURAGE HIM, MASTER TIIN.
GENERAL KENOBI WILL BRIEF YOU ON THE PRIMARY OBJECTIVE...

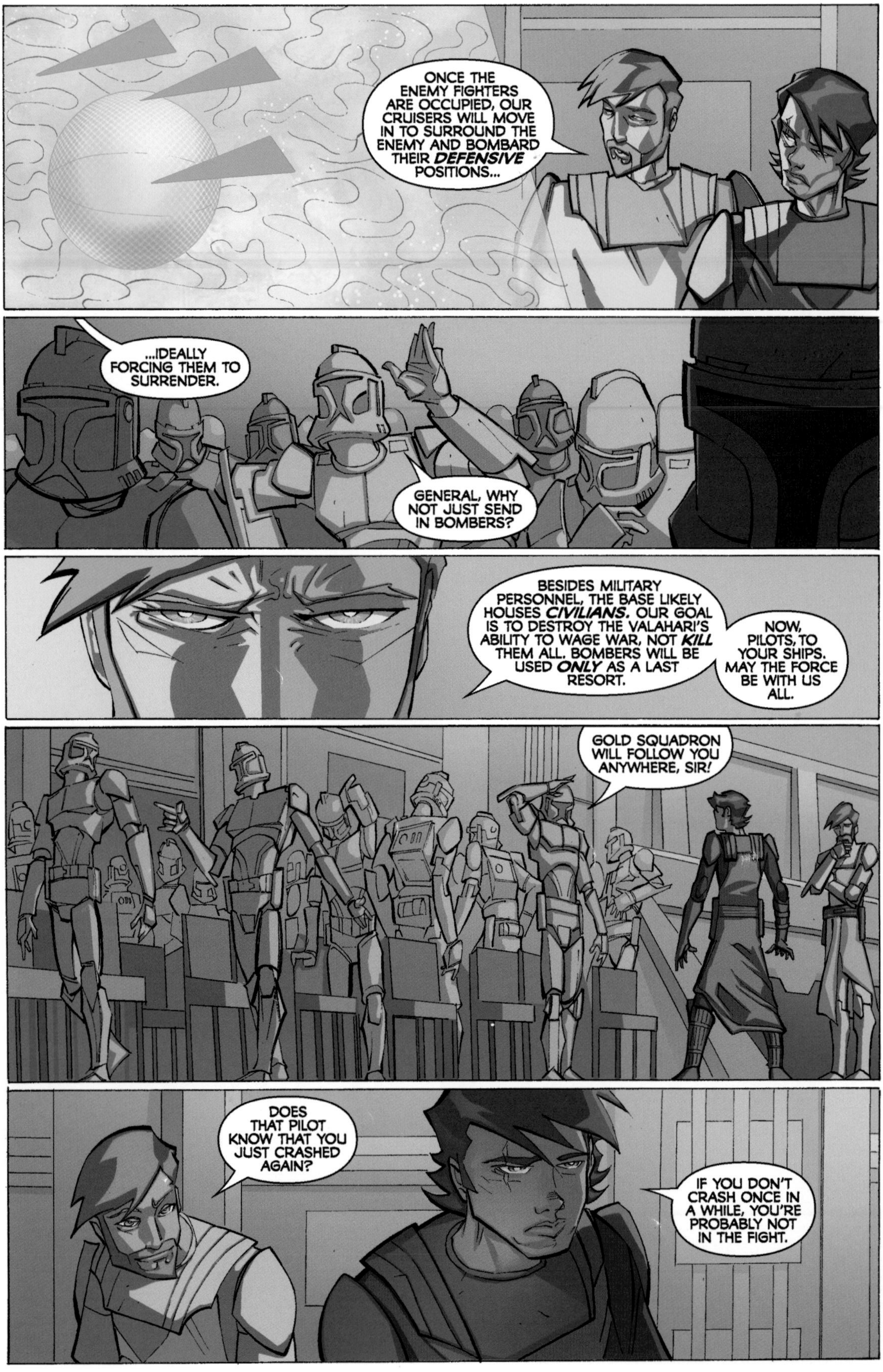
ONCE THE ENEMY FIGHTERS ARE OCCUPIED, OUR CRUISERS WILL MOVE IN TO SURROUND THE ENEMY AND BOMBARD THEIR *DEFENSIVE* POSITIONS...
...IDEALLY FORCING THEM TO SURRENDER.
GENERAL, WHY NOT JUST SEND IN BOMBERS?
BESIDES MILITARY PERSONNEL, THE BASE LIKELY HOUSES *CIVILIANS.* OUR GOAL IS TO DESTROY THE VALAHARI'S ABILITY TO WAGE WAR, NOT *KILL* THEM ALL. BOMBERS WILL BE USED *ONLY* AS A LAST RESORT.
NOW, PILOTS, TO YOUR SHIPS. MAY THE FORCE BE WITH US ALL.
GOLD SQUADRON WILL FOLLOW YOU ANYWHERE, SIR!
DOES THAT PILOT KNOW THAT YOU JUST CRASHED AGAIN?
IF YOU DON'T CRASH ONCE IN A WHILE, YOU'RE PROBABLY NOT IN THE FIGHT.

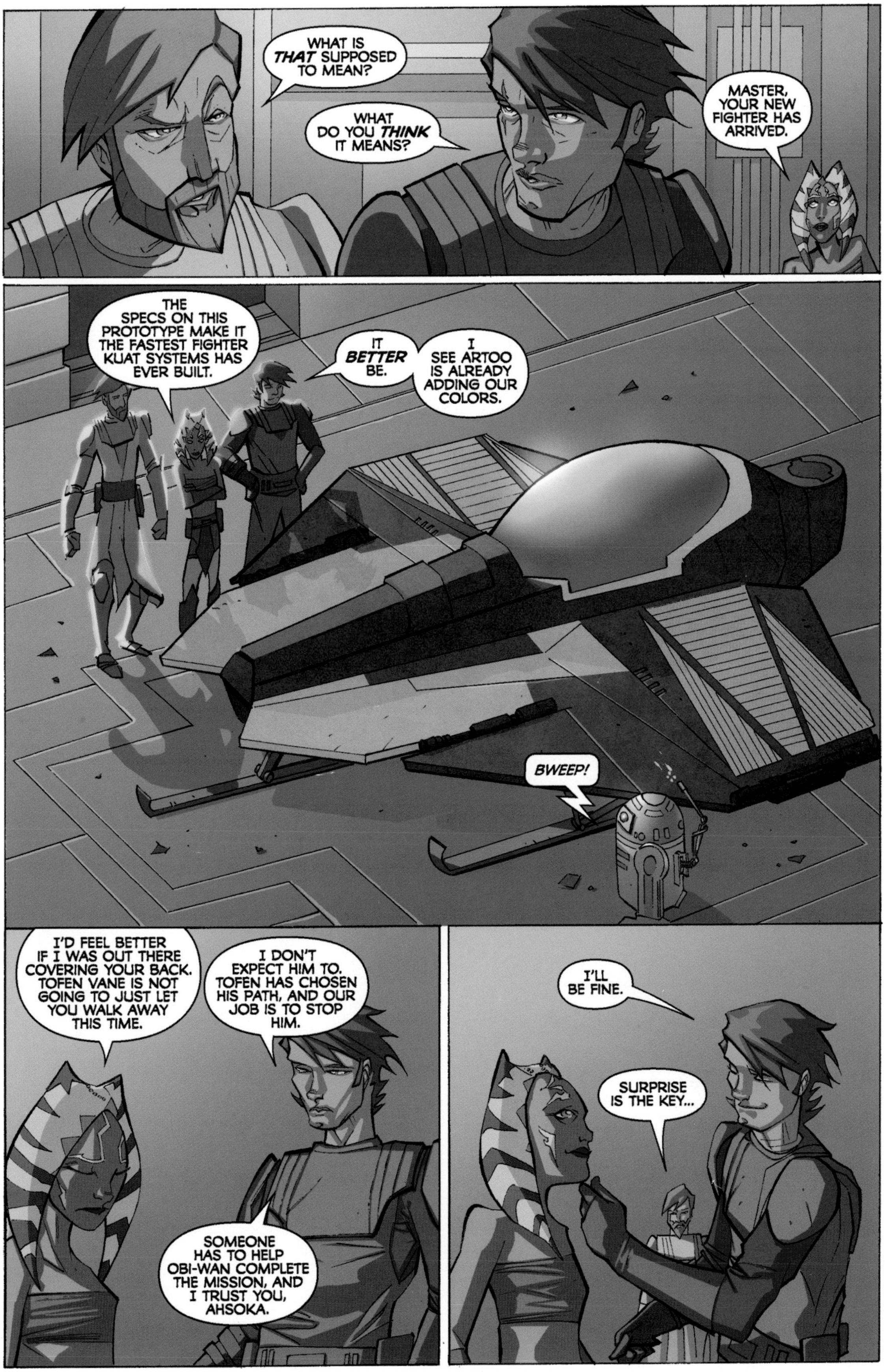
WHAT IS *THAT* SUPPOSED TO MEAN?
WHAT DO YOU *THINK* IT MEANS?
MASTER, YOUR NEW FIGHTER HAS ARRIVED.
THE SPECS ON THIS PROTOTYPE MAKE IT THE FASTEST FIGHTER KUAT SYSTEMS HAS EVER BUILT.
IT *BETTER* BE.
I SEE ARTOO IS ALREADY ADDING OUR COLORS.
BWEEP!
I'D FEEL BETTER IF I WAS OUT THERE COVERING YOUR BACK. TOFEN VANE IS NOT GOING TO JUST LET YOU WALK AWAY THIS TIME.
I DON'T EXPECT HIM TO. TOFEN HAS CHOSEN HIS PATH, AND OUR JOB IS TO STOP HIM.
SOMEONE HAS TO HELP OBI-WAN COMPLETE THE MISSION, AND I TRUST YOU, AHSOKA.
I'LL BE FINE.
SURPRISE IS THE KEY...

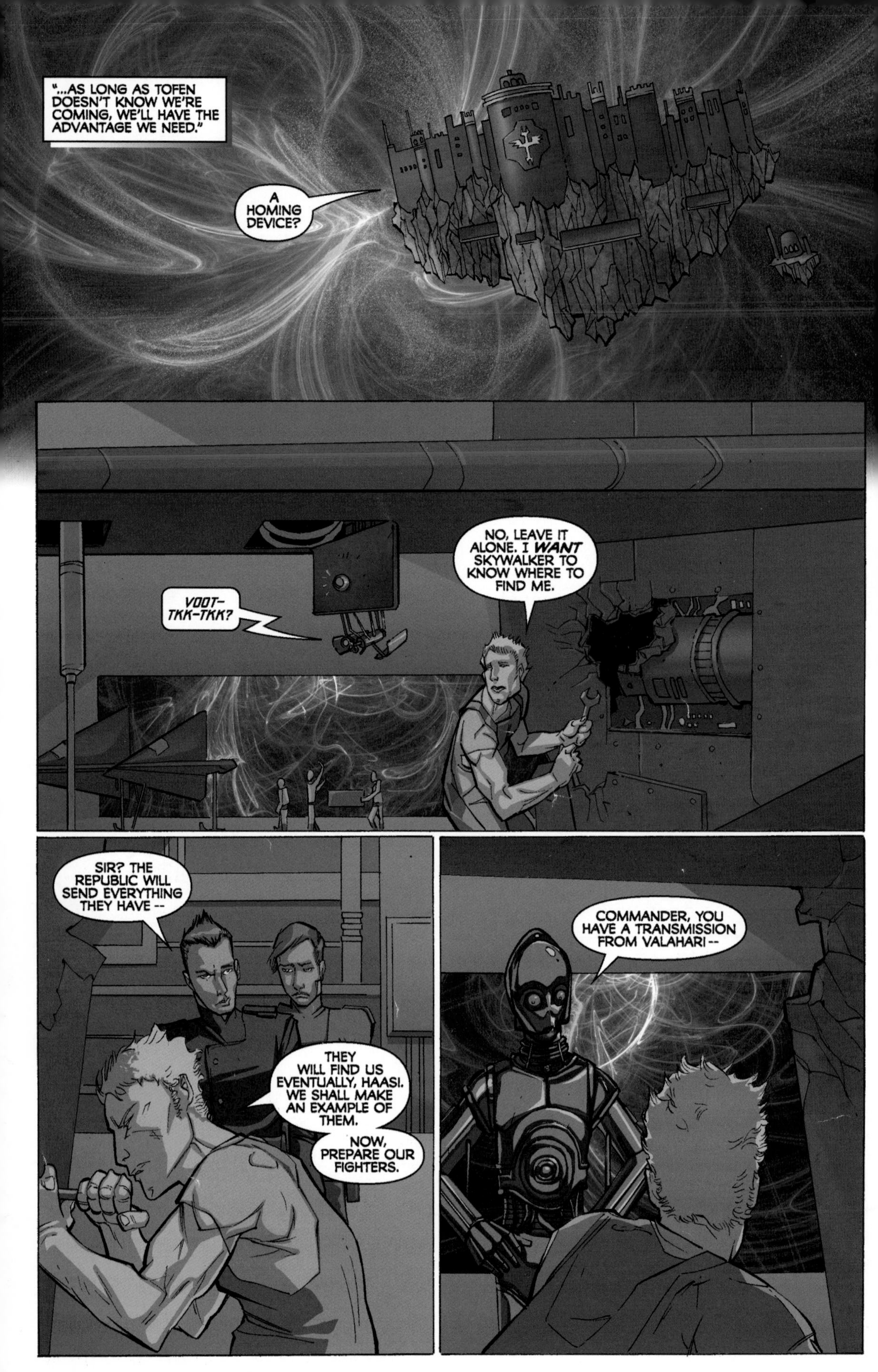
"...AS LONG AS TOFEN DOESN'T KNOW WE'RE COMING, WE'LL HAVE THE ADVANTAGE WE NEED."
A HOMING DEVICE?
VOOT-TKK-TKK?
NO, LEAVE IT ALONE. I *WANT* SKYWALKER TO KNOW WHERE TO FIND ME.
SIR? THE REPUBLIC WILL SEND EVERYTHING THEY HAVE --
THEY WILL FIND US EVENTUALLY, HAASI. WE SHALL MAKE AN EXAMPLE OF THEM.
NOW, PREPARE OUR FIGHTERS.
COMMANDER, YOU HAVE A TRANSMISSION FROM VALAHARI --

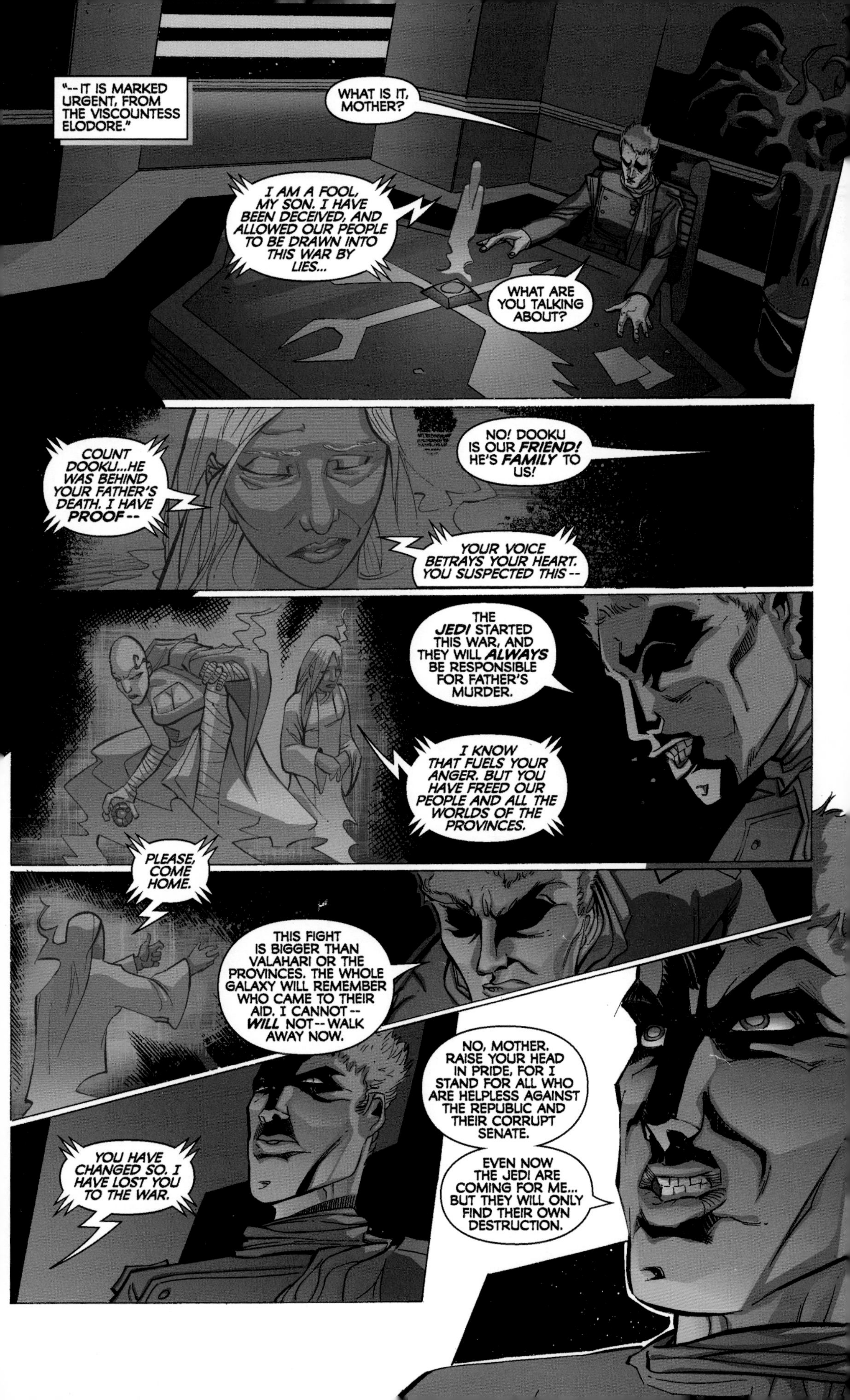
"-- IT IS MARKED URGENT, FROM THE VISCOUNTESS ELODORE."
WHAT IS IT, MOTHER?
I AM A FOOL, MY SON. I HAVE BEEN DECEIVED, AND ALLOWED OUR PEOPLE TO BE DRAWN INTO THIS WAR BY LIES...
WHAT ARE YOU TALKING ABOUT?
COUNT DOOKU...HE WAS BEHIND YOUR FATHER'S DEATH. I HAVE PROOF --
NO! DOOKU IS OUR FRIEND! HE'S FAMILY TO US!
YOUR VOICE BETRAYS YOUR HEART. YOU SUSPECTED THIS --
THE JEDI STARTED THIS WAR, AND THEY WILL ALWAYS BE RESPONSIBLE FOR FATHER'S MURDER.
I KNOW THAT FUELS YOUR ANGER. BUT YOU HAVE FREED OUR PEOPLE AND ALL THE WORLDS OF THE PROVINCES.
PLEASE, COME HOME.
THIS FIGHT IS BIGGER THAN VALAHARI OR THE PROVINCES. THE WHOLE GALAXY WILL REMEMBER WHO CAME TO THEIR AID. I CANNOT -- WILL NOT -- WALK AWAY NOW.
YOU HAVE CHANGED SO. I HAVE LOST YOU TO THE WAR.
NO, MOTHER. RAISE YOUR HEAD IN PRIDE, FOR I STAND FOR ALL WHO ARE HELPLESS AGAINST THE REPUBLIC AND THEIR CORRUPT SENATE.
EVEN NOW THE JEDI ARE COMING FOR ME... BUT THEY WILL ONLY FIND THEIR OWN DESTRUCTION.

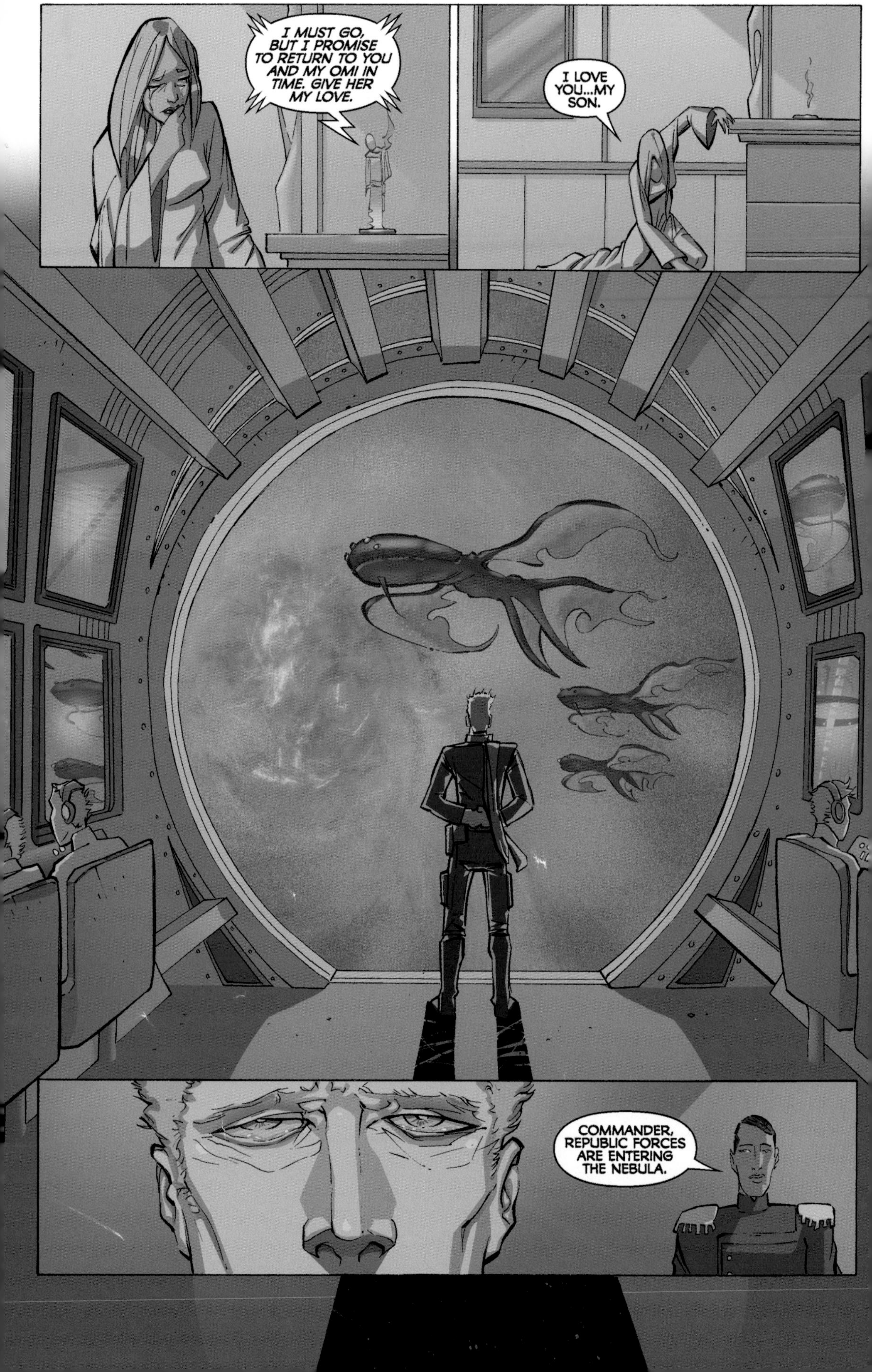
I MUST GO, BUT I PROMISE TO RETURN TO YOU AND MY OMI IN TIME. GIVE HER MY LOVE.
I LOVE YOU...MY SON.
COMMANDER, REPUBLIC FORCES ARE ENTERING THE NEBULA.

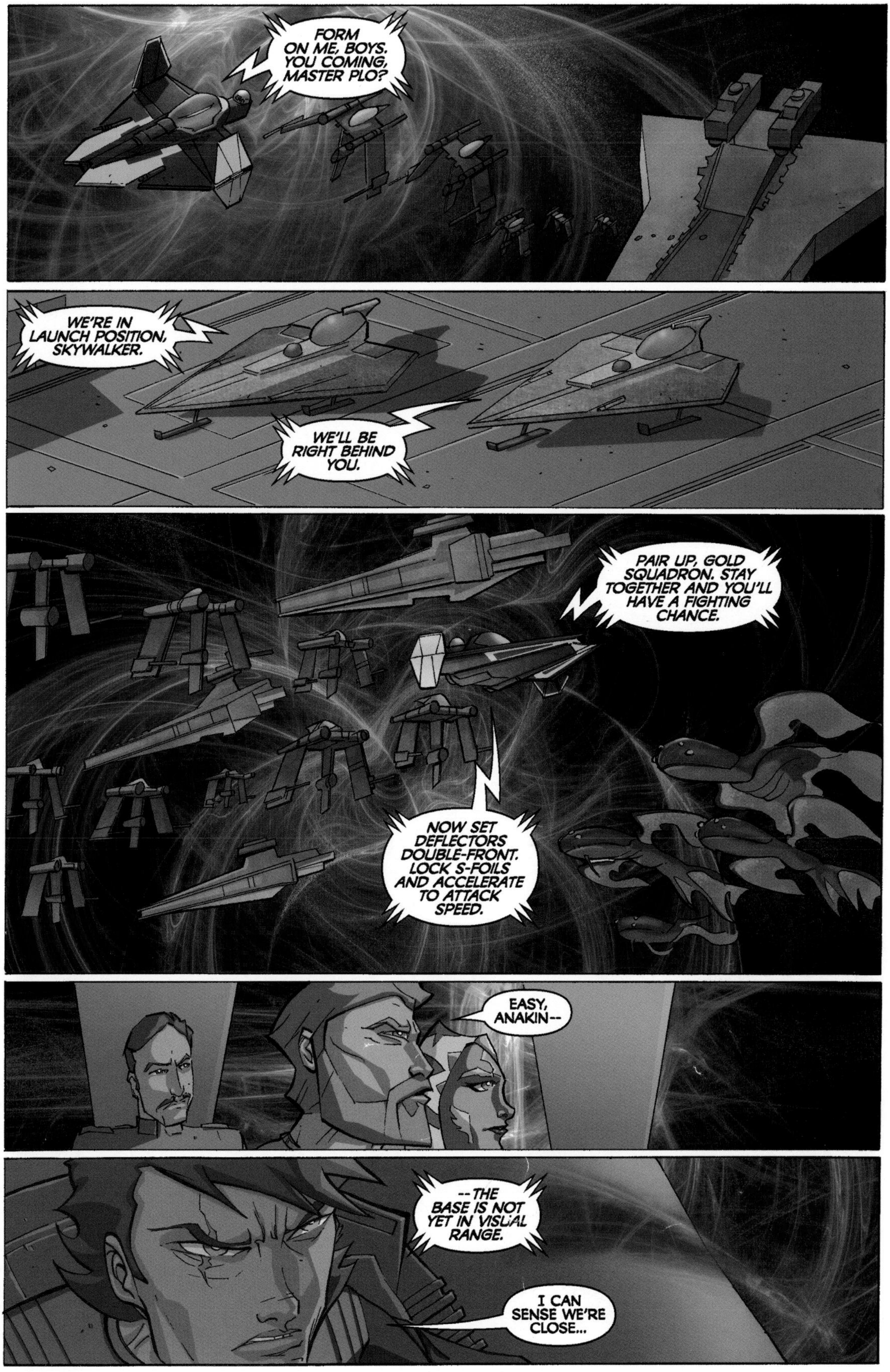
FORM ON ME, BOYS. YOU COMING, MASTER PLO?
WE'RE IN LAUNCH POSITION, SKYWALKER.
WE'LL BE RIGHT BEHIND YOU.
PAIR UP, GOLD SQUADRON. STAY TOGETHER AND YOU'LL HAVE A FIGHTING CHANCE.
NOW SET DEFLECTORS DOUBLE-FRONT. LOCK S-FOILS AND ACCELERATE TO ATTACK SPEED.
EASY, ANAKIN--
--THE BASE IS NOT YET IN VISUAL RANGE.
I CAN SENSE WE'RE CLOSE...

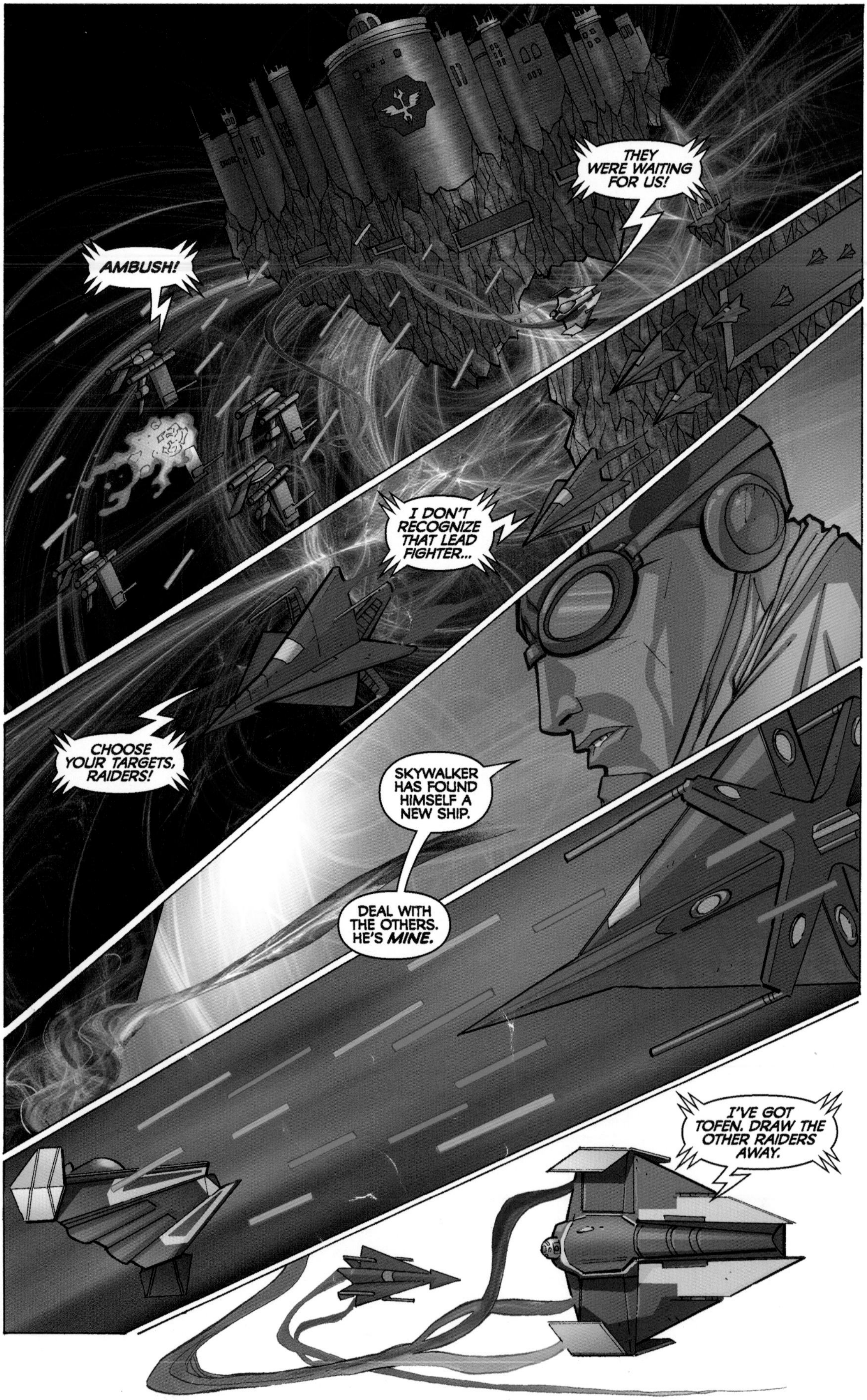
THEY WERE WAITING FOR US!
AMBUSH!
I DON'T RECOGNIZE THAT LEAD FIGHTER...
CHOOSE YOUR TARGETS, RAIDERS!
SKYWALKER HAS FOUND HIMSELF A NEW SHIP.
DEAL WITH THE OTHERS. HE'S *MINE.*
I'VE GOT TOFEN. DRAW THE OTHER RAIDERS AWAY.

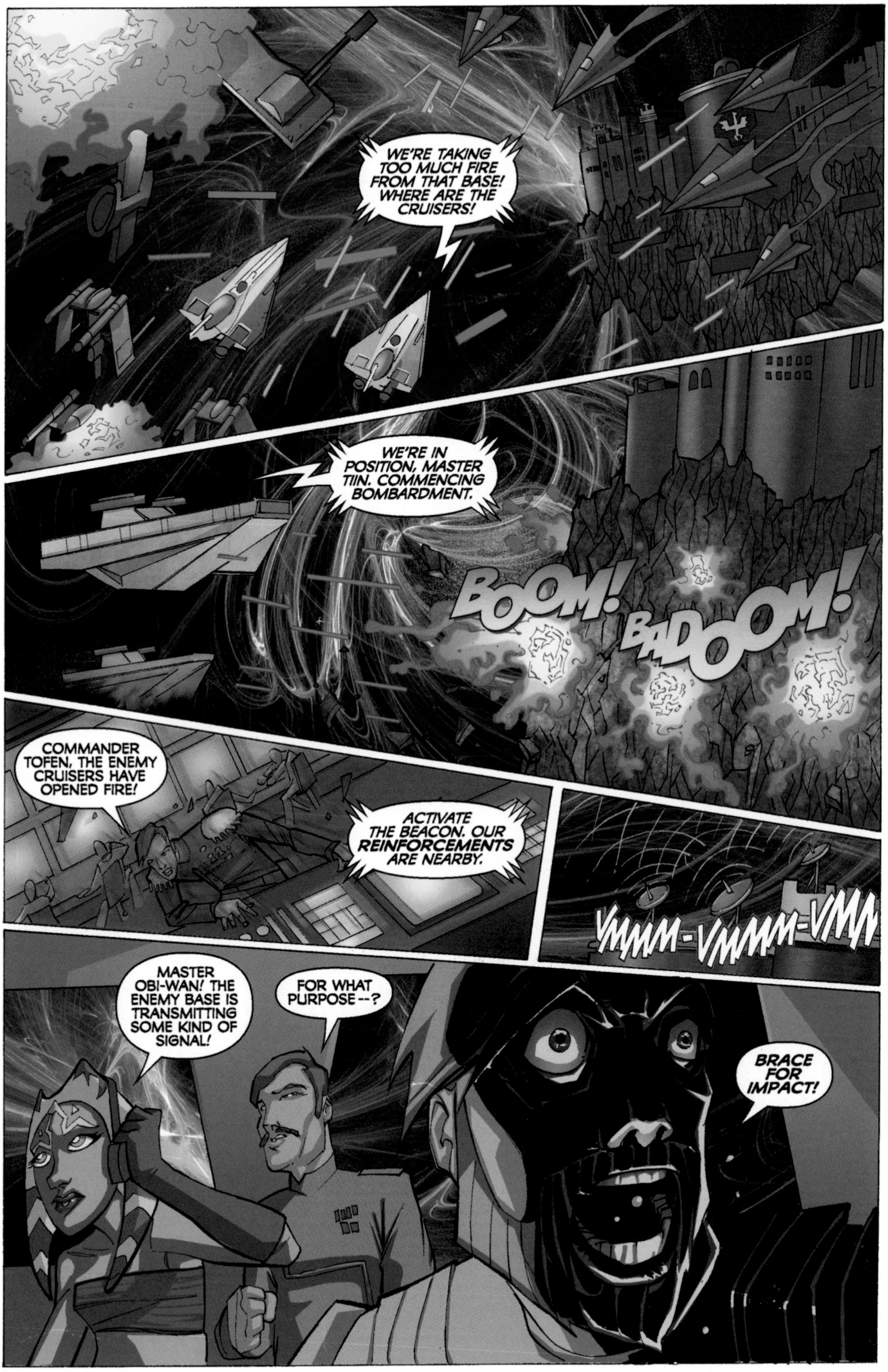
WE'RE TAKING TOO MUCH FIRE FROM THAT BASE! WHERE ARE THE CRUISERS!
WE'RE IN POSITION, MASTER TIIN. COMMENCING BOMBARDMENT.
BOOM! BADOOOM!
COMMANDER TOFEN, THE ENEMY CRUISERS HAVE OPENED FIRE!
ACTIVATE THE BEACON. OUR REINFORCEMENTS ARE NEARBY.
VMMM-VMMM-VMM
MASTER OBI-WAN! THE ENEMY BASE IS TRANSMITTING SOME KIND OF SIGNAL!
FOR WHAT PURPOSE--?
BRACE FOR IMPACT!

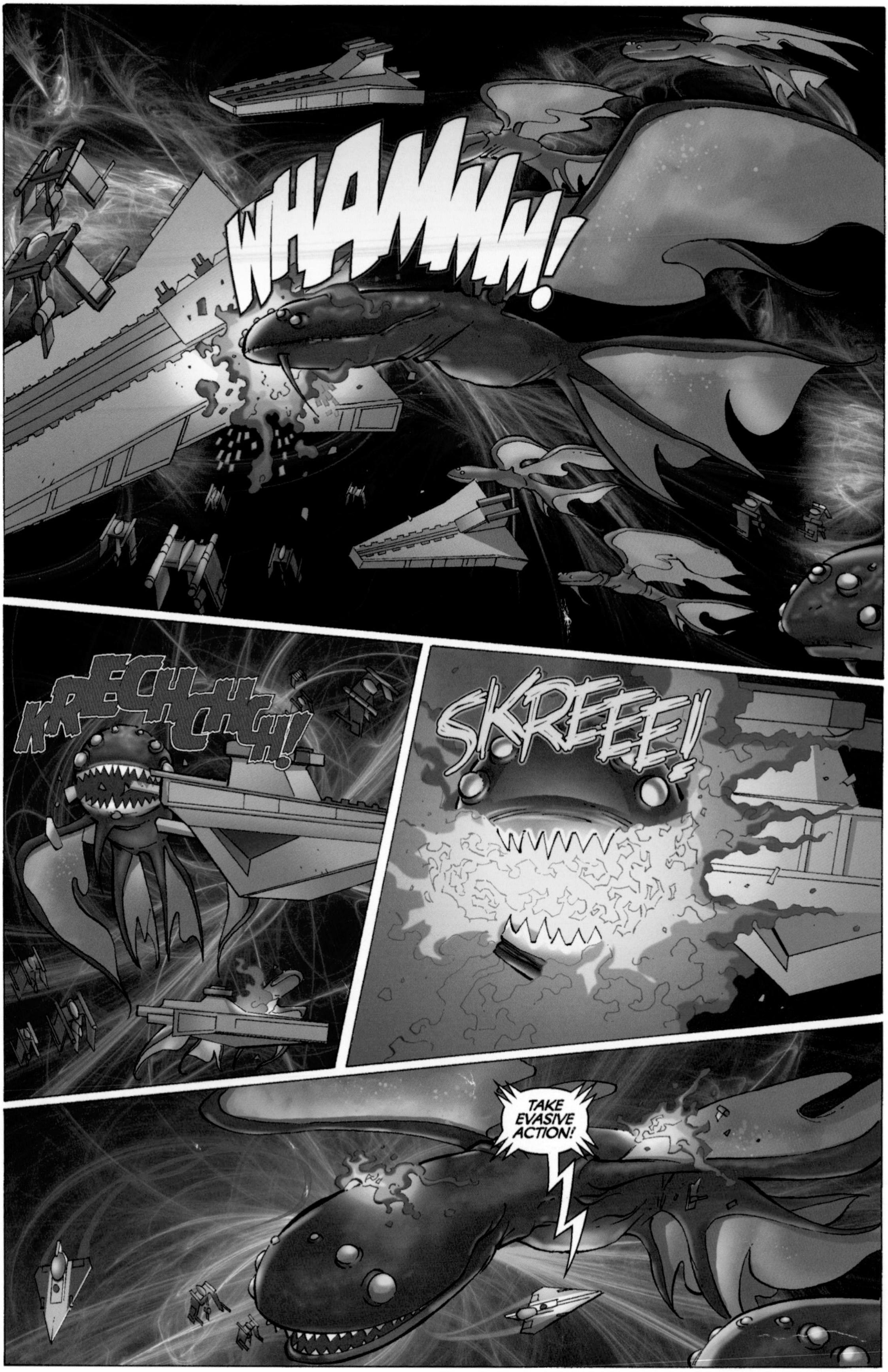
WHAMMM!
SKREEE!
TAKE EVASIVE ACTION!

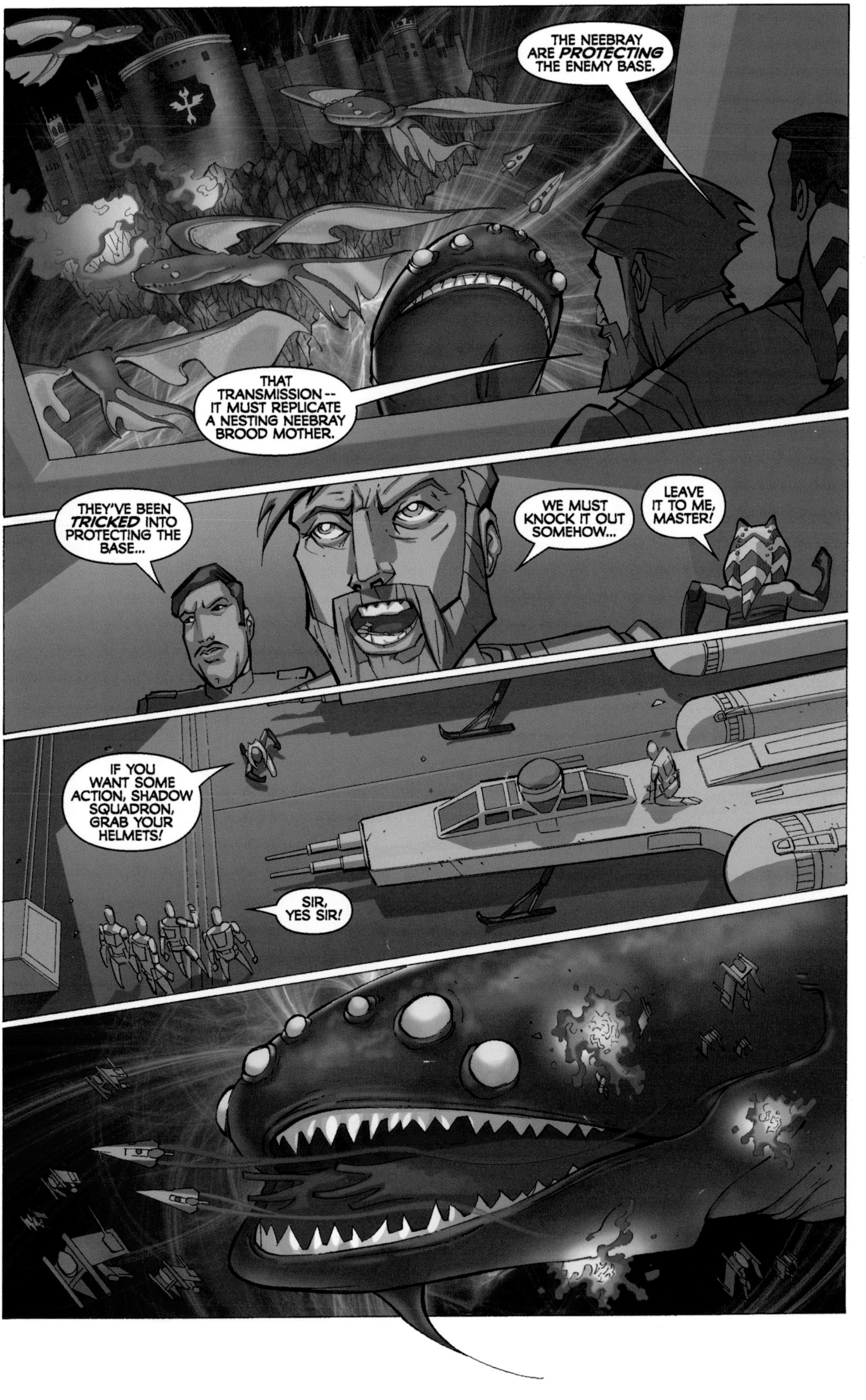
THE NEEBRAY ARE PROTECTING THE ENEMY BASE.
THAT TRANSMISSION -- IT MUST REPLICATE A NESTING NEEBRAY BROOD MOTHER.
THEY'VE BEEN TRICKED INTO PROTECTING THE BASE...
WE MUST KNOCK IT OUT SOMEHOW...
LEAVE IT TO ME, MASTER!
IF YOU WANT SOME ACTION, SHADOW SQUADRON, GRAB YOUR HELMETS!
SIR, YES SIR!

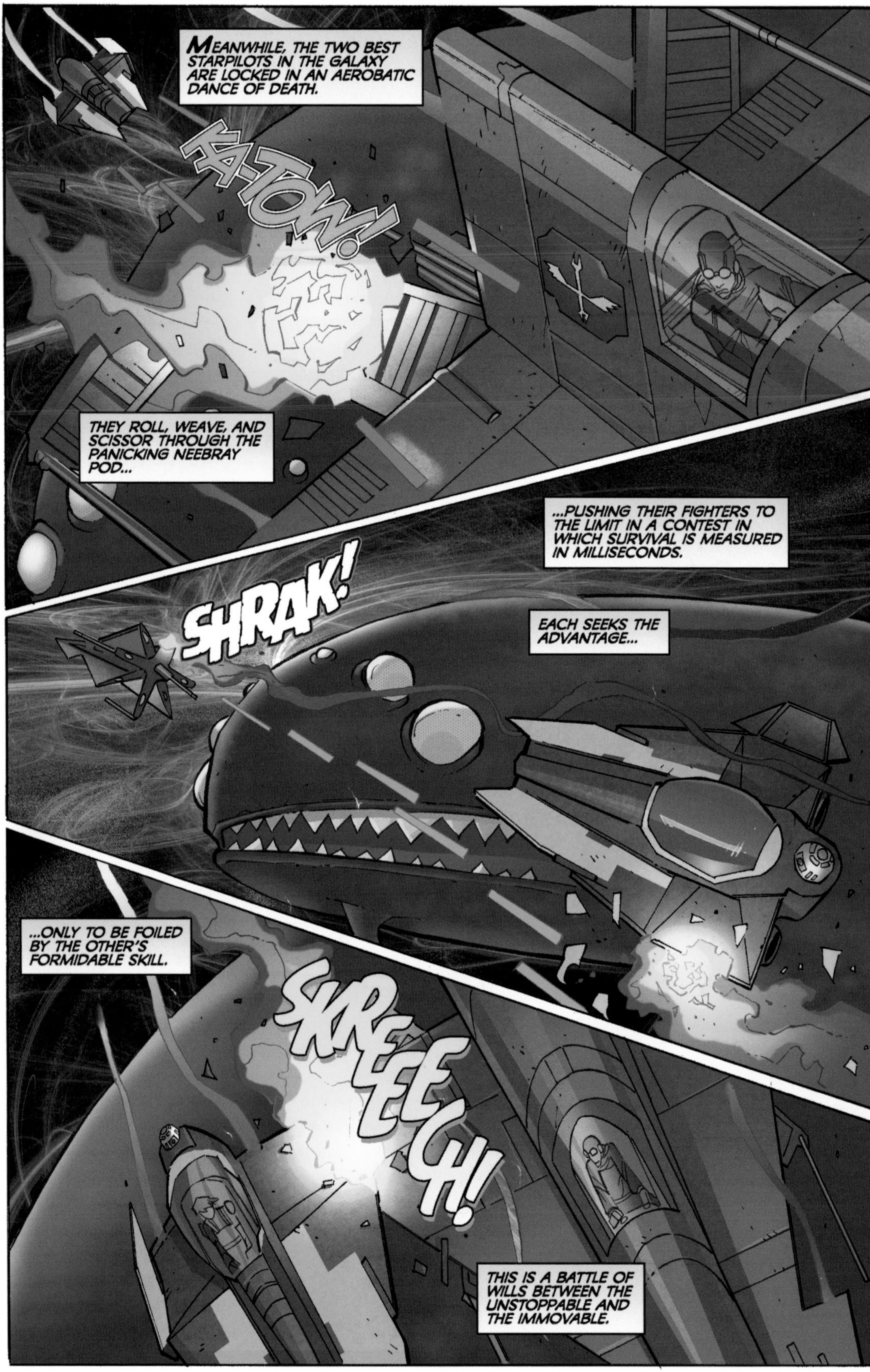
MEANWHILE, THE TWO BEST STARPILOTS IN THE GALAXY ARE LOCKED IN AN AEROBATIC DANCE OF DEATH.
KA-TOW!
THEY ROLL, WEAVE, AND SCISSOR THROUGH THE PANICKING NEEBRAY POD...
...PUSHING THEIR FIGHTERS TO THE LIMIT IN A CONTEST IN WHICH SURVIVAL IS MEASURED IN MILLISECONDS.
SHRAK!
EACH SEEKS THE ADVANTAGE...
...ONLY TO BE FOILED BY THE OTHER'S FORMIDABLE SKILL.
SKREEEECH!
THIS IS A BATTLE OF WILLS BETWEEN THE UNSTOPPABLE AND THE IMMOVABLE.

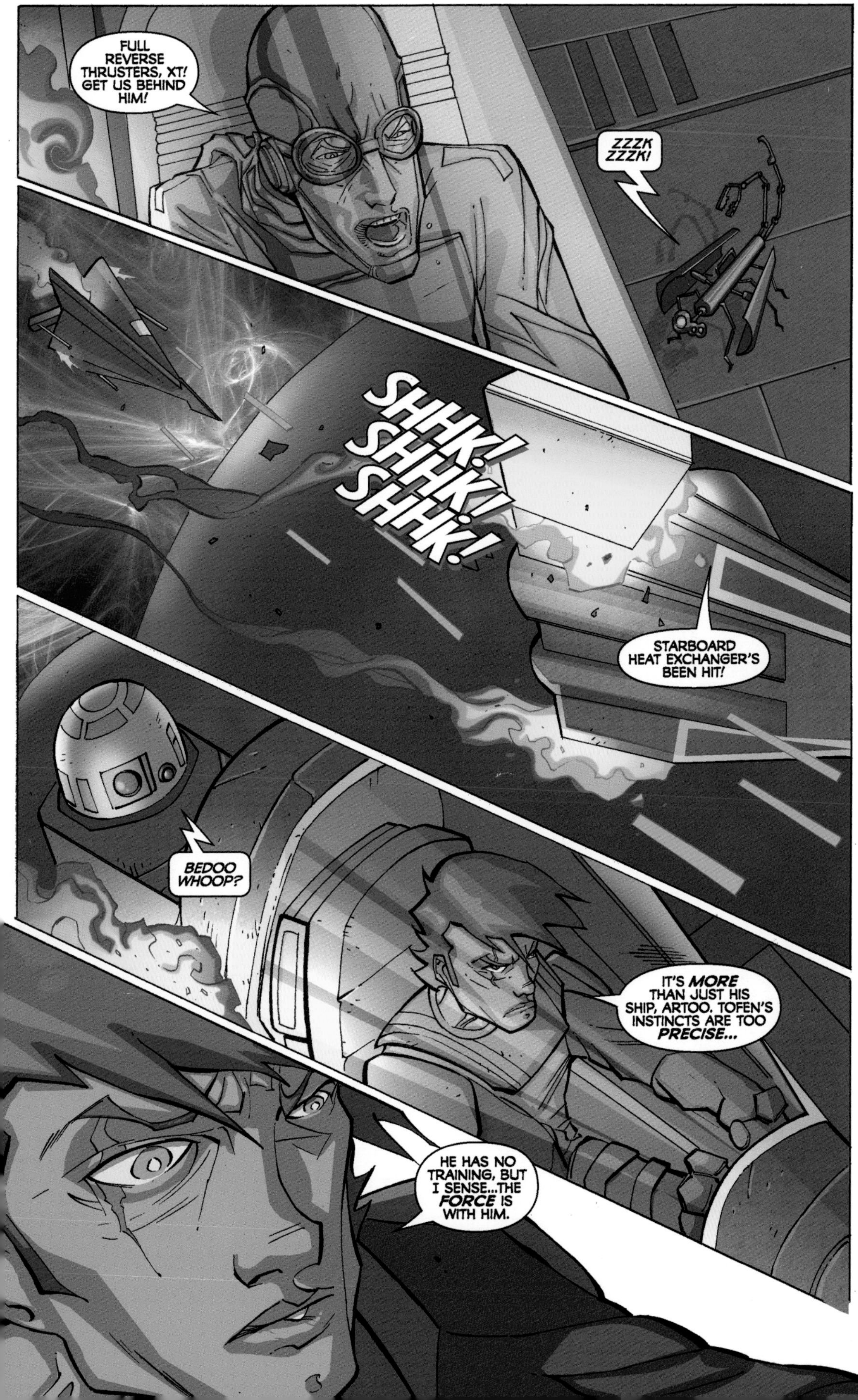
FULL REVERSE THRUSTERS, XT! GET US BEHIND HIM!
ZZZK ZZZK!
SHHK! SHHK! SHHK!
STARBOARD HEAT EXCHANGER'S BEEN HIT!
BEDOO WHOOP?
IT'S *MORE* THAN JUST HIS SHIP, ARTOO. TOFEN'S INSTINCTS ARE TOO *PRECISE...*
HE HAS NO TRAINING, BUT I SENSE...THE *FORCE* IS WITH HIM.

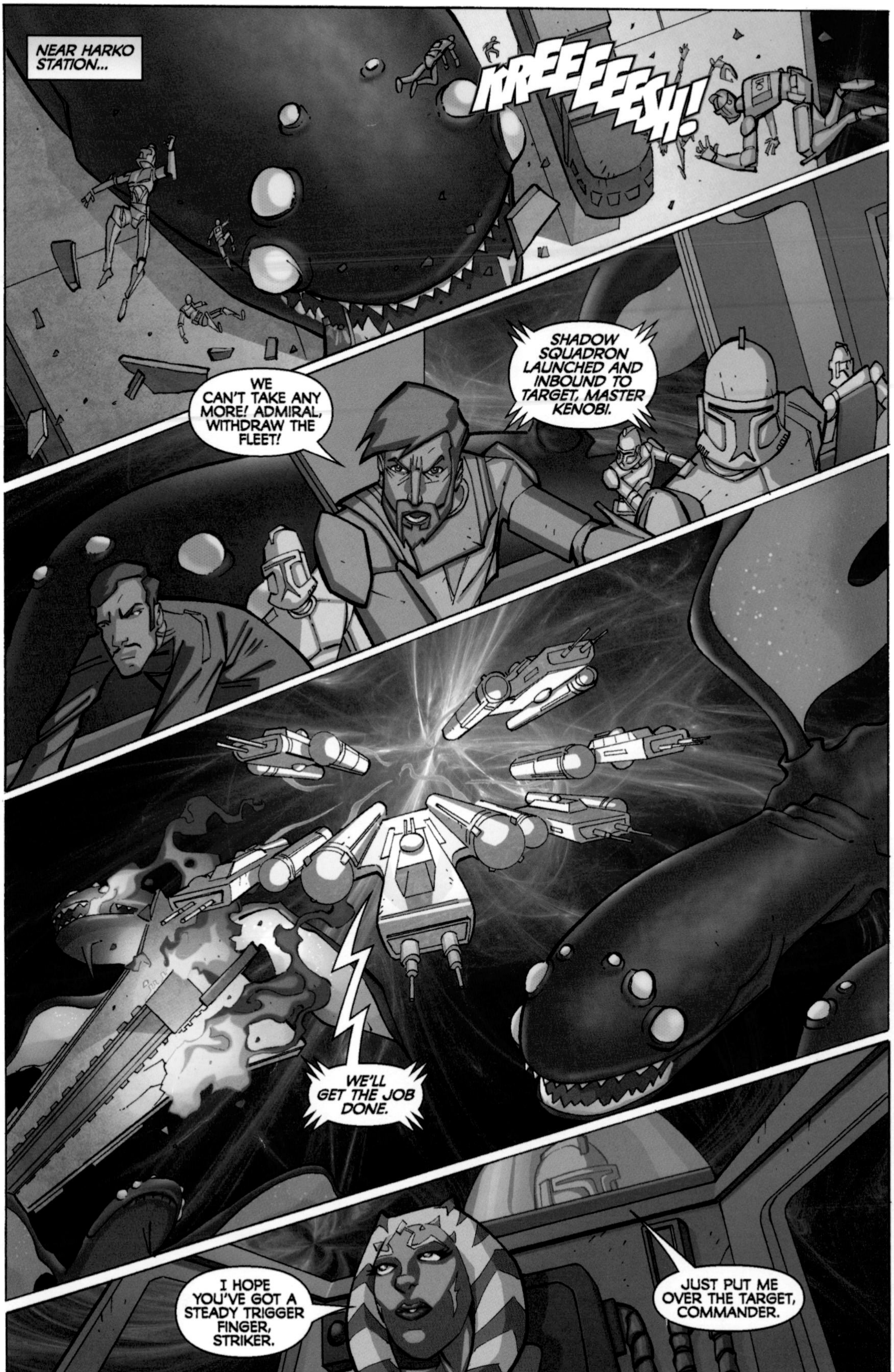
NEAR HARKO STATION...
KREEEEEESH!
WE CAN'T TAKE ANY MORE! ADMIRAL, WITHDRAW THE FLEET!
SHADOW SQUADRON LAUNCHED AND INBOUND TO TARGET, MASTER KENOBI.
WE'LL GET THE JOB DONE.
I HOPE YOU'VE GOT A STEADY TRIGGER FINGER, STRIKER.
JUST PUT ME OVER THE TARGET, COMMANDER.

AHSOKA, WE SIGNALED OUR INTENT IN ACCORDANCE WITH THE CONVENTION. THEY'VE HAD THEIR CHANCE TO EVACUATE. BEGIN YOUR BOMBING RUN!

YES, MASTER.

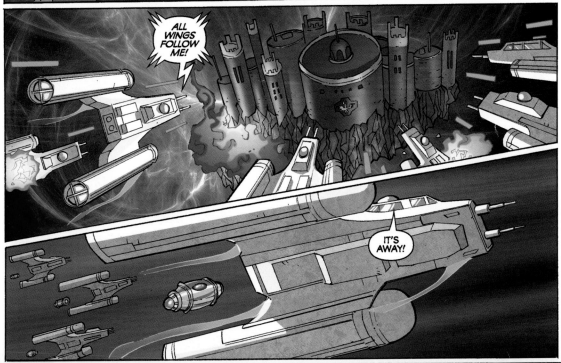

ALL WINGS FOLLOW ME!

IT'S AWAY!

GENERAL, SHE DID IT! THE NEEBRAY ARE DISPERSING.

SEND OUT RESCUE SHIPS. SEARCH THE DEBRIS FOR LIFEPODS.

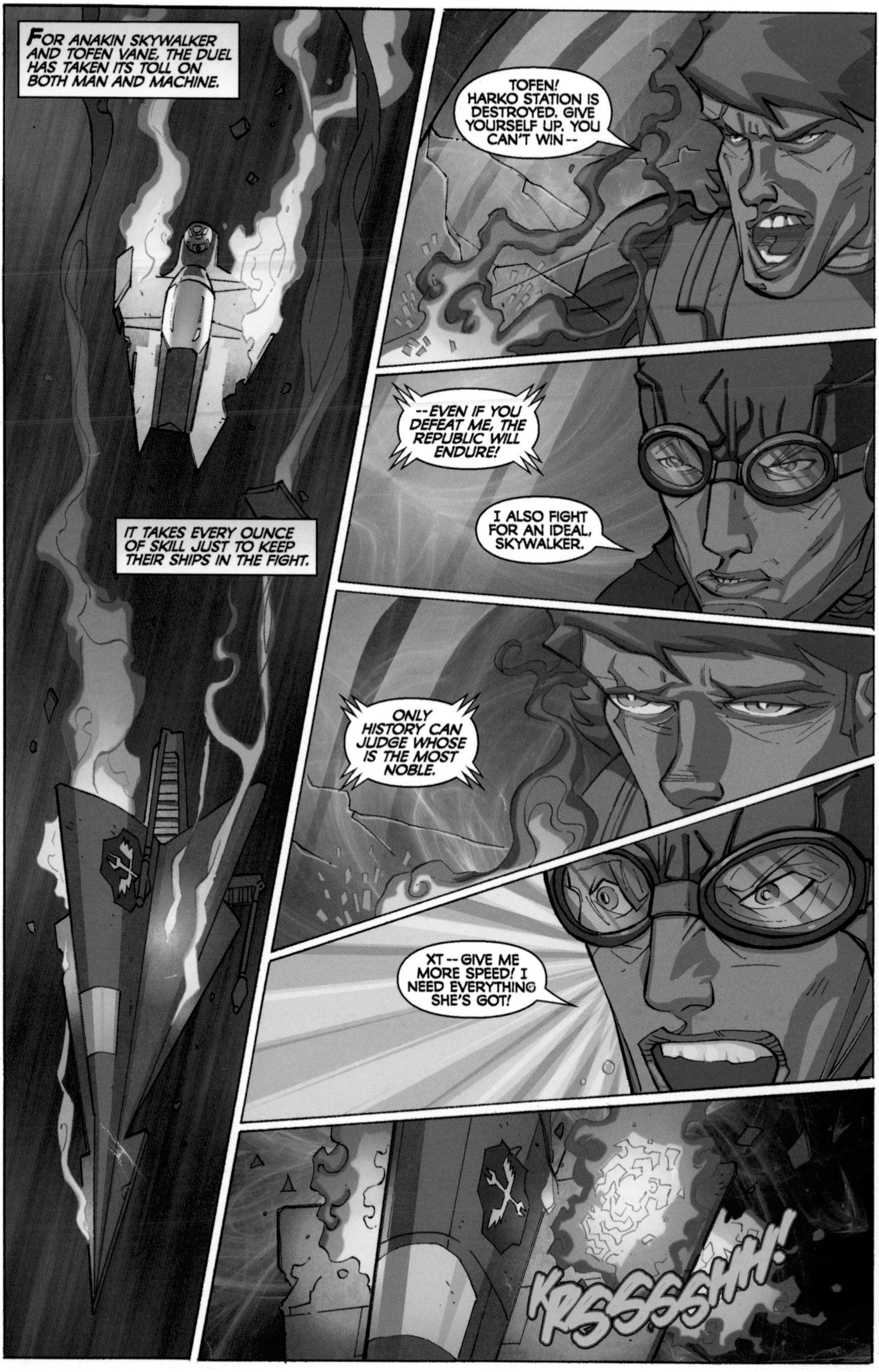
FOR ANAKIN SKYWALKER AND TOFEN VANE, THE DUEL HAS TAKEN ITS TOLL ON BOTH MAN AND MACHINE.
TOFEN! HARKO STATION IS DESTROYED. GIVE YOURSELF UP. YOU CAN'T WIN--
--EVEN IF YOU DEFEAT ME, THE REPUBLIC WILL ENDURE!
I ALSO FIGHT FOR AN IDEAL, SKYWALKER.
IT TAKES EVERY OUNCE OF SKILL JUST TO KEEP THEIR SHIPS IN THE FIGHT.
ONLY HISTORY CAN JUDGE WHOSE IS THE MOST NOBLE.
XT--GIVE ME MORE SPEED! I NEED EVERYTHING SHE'S GOT!
KRSSSSHH!

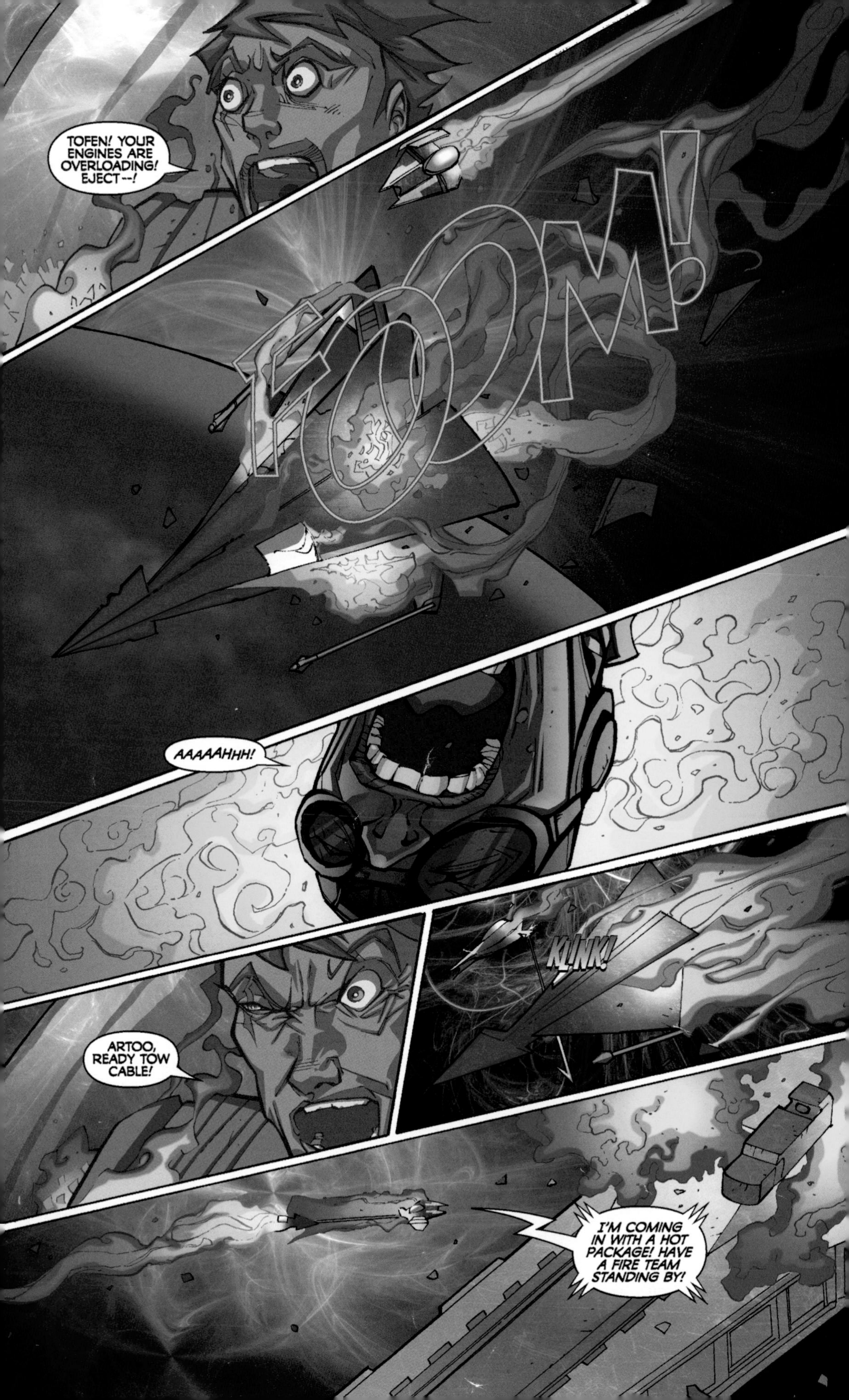
TOFEN! YOUR ENGINES ARE OVERLOADING! EJECT--!
FOOM!
AAAAAHHH!
KLINK!
ARTOO, READY TOW CABLE!
I'M COMING IN WITH A HOT PACKAGE! HAVE A FIRE TEAM STANDING BY!

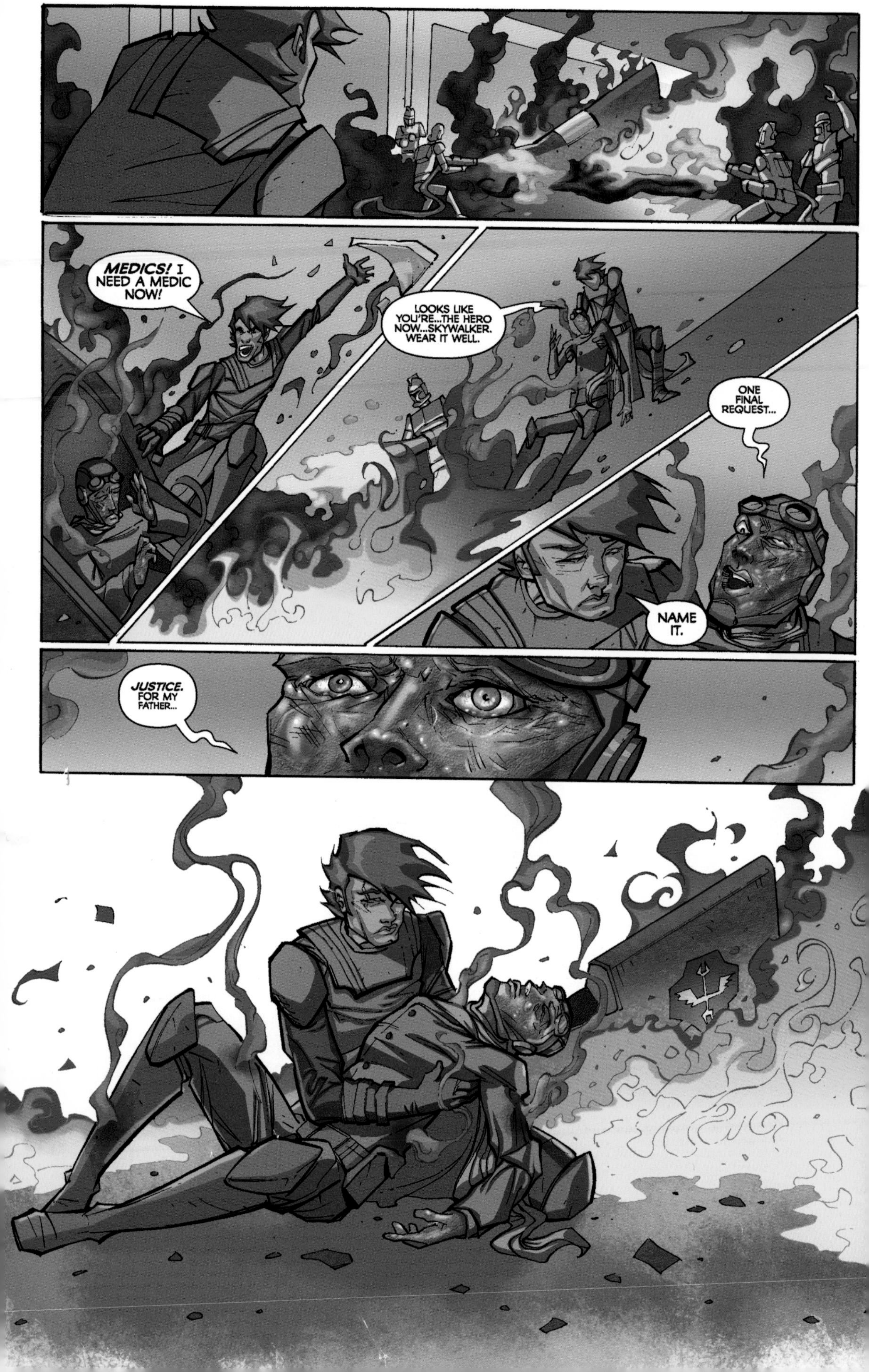
MEDICS! I NEED A MEDIC NOW!
LOOKS LIKE YOU'RE...THE HERO NOW...SKYWALKER. WEAR IT WELL.
ONE FINAL REQUEST...
NAME IT.
JUSTICE. FOR MY FATHER...

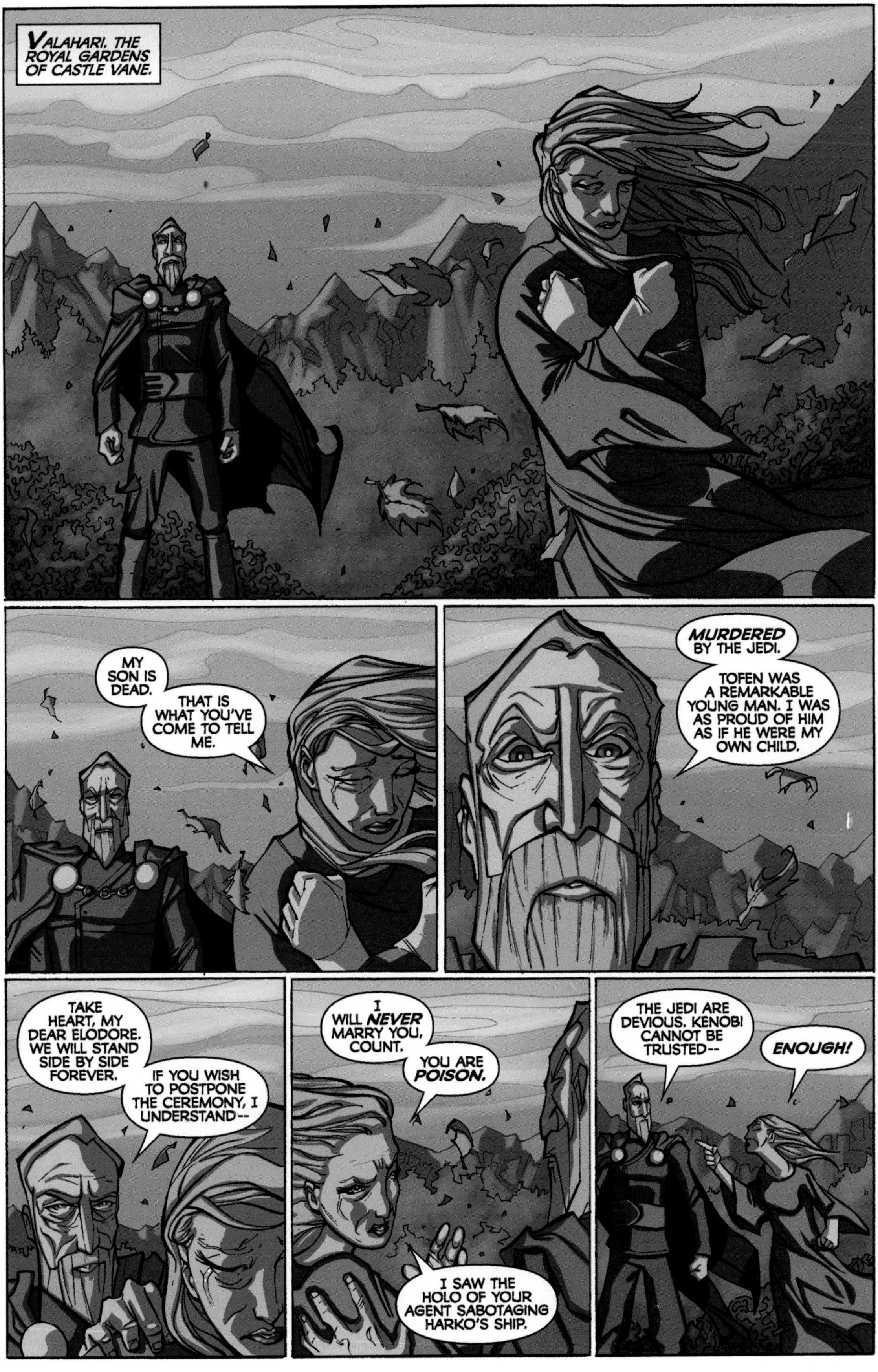
VALAHARI. THE ROYAL GARDENS OF CASTLE VANE.
MY SON IS DEAD.
THAT IS WHAT YOU'VE COME TO TELL ME.
MURDERED BY THE JEDI.
TOFEN WAS A REMARKABLE YOUNG MAN. I WAS AS PROUD OF HIM AS IF HE WERE MY OWN CHILD.
TAKE HEART, MY DEAR ELODORE. WE WILL STAND SIDE BY SIDE FOREVER.
IF YOU WISH TO POSTPONE THE CEREMONY, I UNDERSTAND--
I WILL NEVER MARRY YOU, COUNT.
YOU ARE POISON.
I SAW THE HOLO OF YOUR AGENT SABOTAGING HARKO'S SHIP.
THE JEDI ARE DEVIOUS. KENOBI CANNOT BE TRUSTED--
ENOUGH!

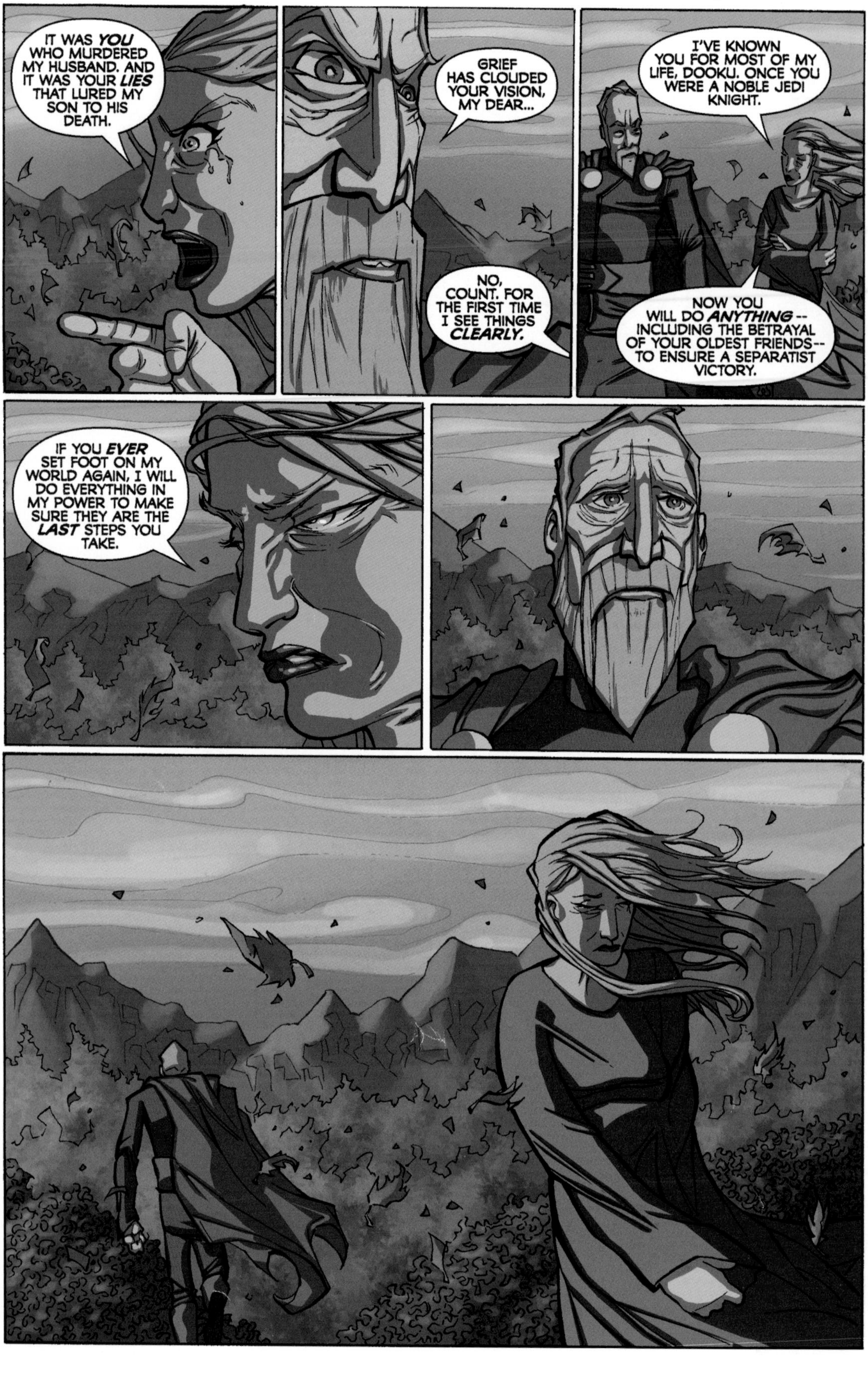
IT WAS YOU WHO MURDERED MY HUSBAND. AND IT WAS YOUR LIES THAT LURED MY SON TO HIS DEATH.
GRIEF HAS CLOUDED YOUR VISION, MY DEAR...
NO, COUNT. FOR THE FIRST TIME I SEE THINGS CLEARLY.
I'VE KNOWN YOU FOR MOST OF MY LIFE, DOOKU. ONCE YOU WERE A NOBLE JEDI KNIGHT.
NOW YOU WILL DO ANYTHING -- INCLUDING THE BETRAYAL OF YOUR OLDEST FRIENDS-- TO ENSURE A SEPARATIST VICTORY.
IF YOU EVER SET FOOT ON MY WORLD AGAIN, I WILL DO EVERYTHING IN MY POWER TO MAKE SURE THEY ARE THE LAST STEPS YOU TAKE.

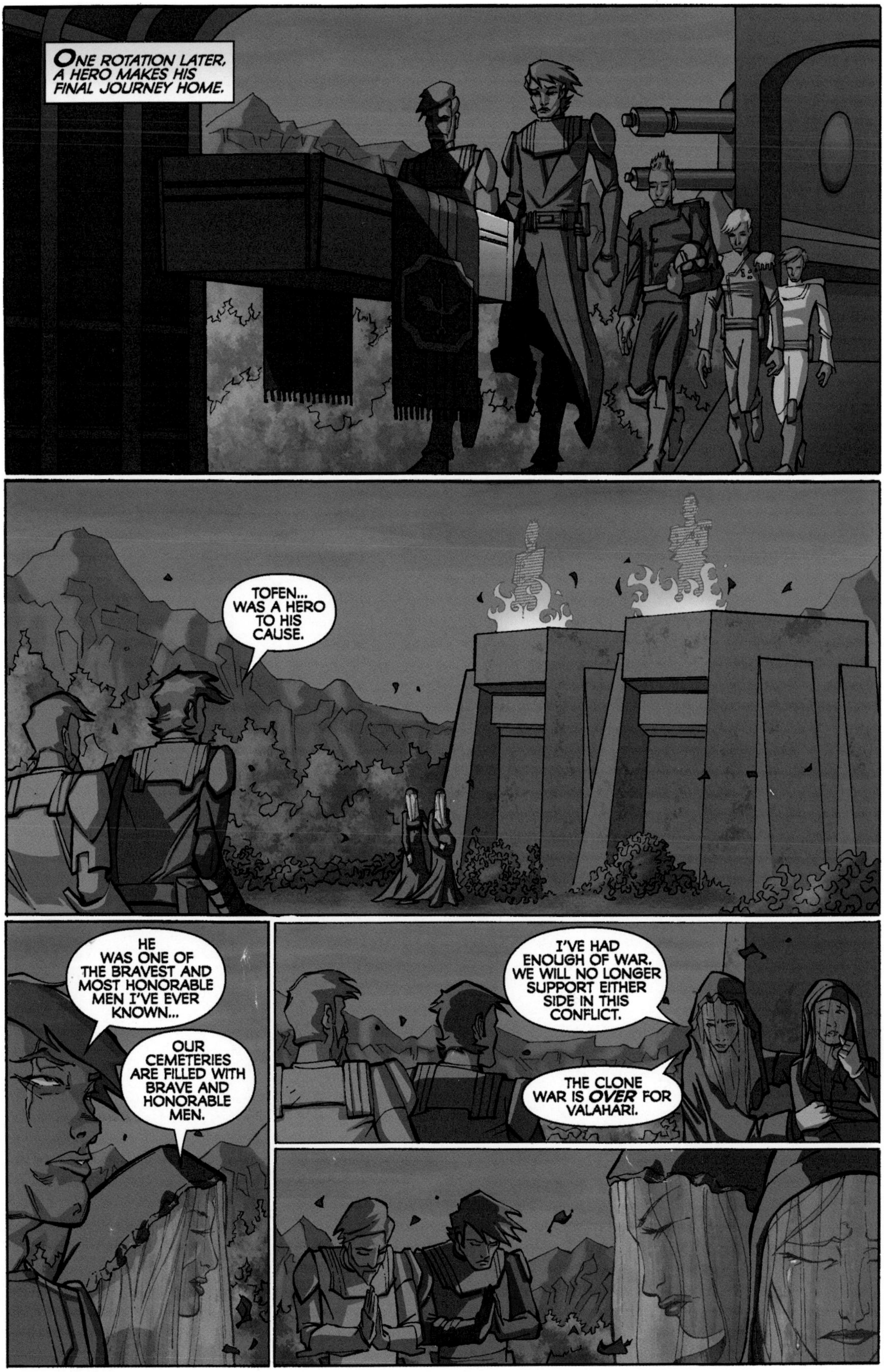

ONE ROTATION LATER, A HERO MAKES HIS FINAL JOURNEY HOME.
TOFEN... WAS A HERO TO HIS CAUSE.
HE WAS ONE OF THE BRAVEST AND MOST HONORABLE MEN I'VE EVER KNOWN...
OUR CEMETERIES ARE FILLED WITH BRAVE AND HONORABLE MEN.
I'VE HAD ENOUGH OF WAR. WE WILL NO LONGER SUPPORT EITHER SIDE IN THIS CONFLICT.
THE CLONE WAR IS OVER FOR VALAHARI.

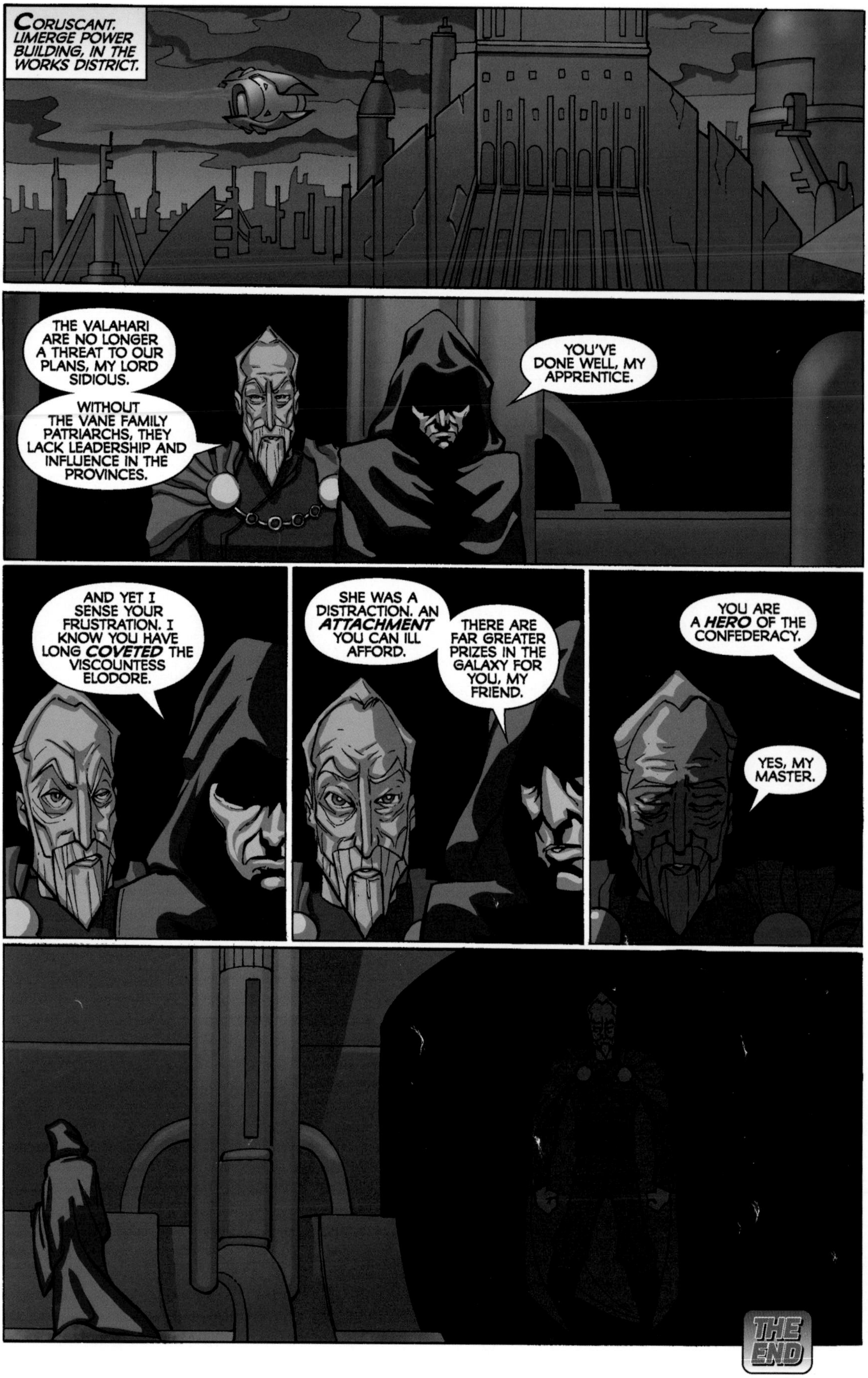
CORUSCANT. LIMERGE POWER BUILDING, IN THE WORKS DISTRICT.
THE VALAHARI ARE NO LONGER A THREAT TO OUR PLANS, MY LORD SIDIOUS.
WITHOUT THE VANE FAMILY PATRIARCHS, THEY LACK LEADERSHIP AND INFLUENCE IN THE PROVINCES.
YOU'VE DONE WELL, MY APPRENTICE.
AND YET I SENSE YOUR FRUSTRATION. I KNOW YOU HAVE LONG *COVETED* THE VISCOUNTESS ELODORE.
SHE WAS A DISTRACTION. AN *ATTACHMENT* YOU CAN ILL AFFORD.
THERE ARE FAR GREATER PRIZES IN THE GALAXY FOR YOU, MY FRIEND.
YOU ARE A *HERO* OF THE CONFEDERACY.
YES, MY MASTER.
THE END

9/13